Published by Oren Village, LLC, Battle Creek, Michigan. For information or permission to reproduce, please contact author@alanstjean.com or write to Alan St. Jean, PO Box 1, Battle Creek, Michigan 49016. Text set in Baskerville. Cover design by Libby Carruth Krock. Illustrations were rendered in watercolor and pencil.

PUBLISHER'S CATALOGING-IN-PUBLICATION DATA

St. Jean, Alan.

Alyssa and the spider / written by Alan St. Jean ; illustrated by Libby Carruth Krock
1st ed. -- Battle Creek, Mich. : Oren Village, c2009.

p. ; cm.

(The daydreams collection ; v. 3)

ISBN: 978-0-9777272-5-4
Audience: grades K-5.
Summary: Ralphie would much rather watch TV than play with his little sister and her dolls, until a spider shows up and changes everything!

1. Brothers and sisters--Juvenile fiction. 2. Spiders--Juvenile fiction. 3. [Brothers and sisters--Fiction. 4. Spiders--Fiction. 5. Stories in rhyme.] 6. Stories in rhyme. I. Krock, Libby Carruth. II. Title. III. Series.

Printed in Korea

PZ7.S14245 A49 2009
[Fic]--dc22   0908

For Hope, my sweet little sister.
I hope this makes up for all of the times I tormented
you as we were growing up. Oh, the food wars,
I shall never forget...

-Alan St. Jean

ALYSSA and the SPIDER

The Daydreams Collection

Volume III

By Alan St. Jean   Illustrated by Libby Carruth Krock

School's out for the summer,
Ralphie's huddled on the couch.
"Vacation's here!" he giggled
As he found a comfy crouch.

"I'll watch TV, I'll play some games,
I'll tumble on the floor...
And when the scary movie starts
I'll watch TV some more!"

"Ralphie!" called his sister
As she danced into the room.
"Look who wants to play with you,
It's Jibby, Jack and Jume!"

"Alyssa…" Ralphie shook his head,
"Can't you see I'm busy?
You know that boys don't play with dolls!"
He said all in a tizzy.

"But, Ralphie," said Alyssa,
(She was pulling on his sweater)
"I thought you liked to play with me,
I thought you liked me better…"

"…than scary movies on TV,
Than rolling on the floor.
I thought you liked me more than all
The candy at the store."

Ralphie heaved a great big sigh,
He mumbled, "Not today...
The monster movie's gonna start,
So please be on your way."

"And take those goofy looking dolls,
I think one needs an eye.
Your little friends need mending,
Oh please, oh please don't cry!"

Alyssa sadly walked away,
She headed down the hall.
Ralphie grabbed a pillow
And his favorite basketball.

"She'll be fine," he reasoned,
As he stared into the glow.
Then music started playing
From his favorite TV show.

He turned the TV way, way up,
His eyes were getting wider.
"A monster movie!" Ralphie squealed,
"Oh look, a giant spider!"

He pulled the pillow to his face,
Time and time again.
Fear was building up inside,
Ralphie gasped, and then…

"Ralphie!" screamed Alyssa
From her bedroom down the hall.
"Help me, please! Come quickly!
There's a spider on my wall!"

"Wait," pondered Ralphie
As he made a funny smile.
"She's afraid of spiders,
Hmm…I think I'll wait a while."

He headed for the kitchen,
Where he found a tasty fig.
"Ralphie!" called Alyssa,
"Hurry up, it's really big!"

The boy's imagination
Started working overtime.
In his mind he saw
A giant spider, green with slime.

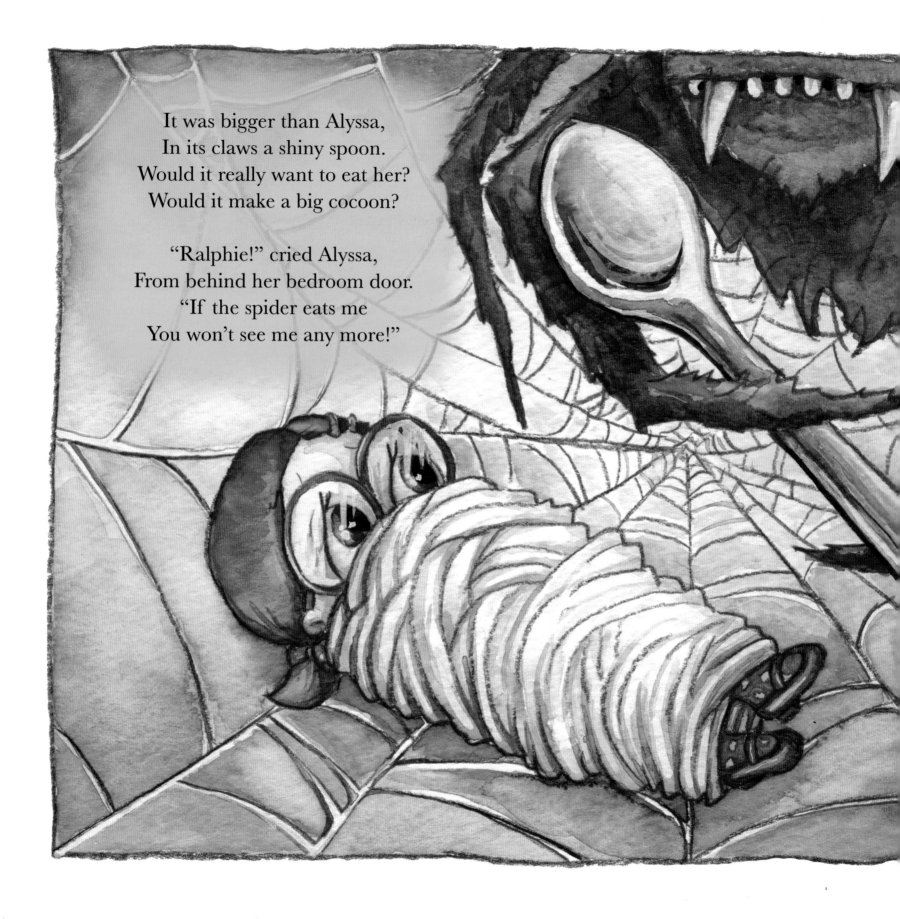

It was bigger than Alyssa,
In its claws a shiny spoon.
Would it really want to eat her?
Would it make a big cocoon?

"Ralphie!" cried Alyssa,
From behind her bedroom door.
"If the spider eats me
You won't see me any more!"

And then, something happened,
Ralphie's laughter disappeared.
He made a funny, pouty face.
He started feeling weird.

A question crossed his mind,
What if Alyssa wasn't there?
He thought about her silly laugh,
He thought about her hair.

He thought about her silly doll,
The one that needs an eye.
"She's the only one that loves her,"
Ralphie sniffed, about to cry.

He hurried down the hall
And burst inside Alyssa's room,
Where he saw a tiny spider
On the handle of a broom.

Then bold determination
Filled his eyes and puffed his chest.
"Ralphie to the rescue!
Lock the door! Let's get this pest!"

"But Ralphie…" said Alyssa,
As she turned to lock the door.
"Not now!" he laughed and giggled,
"Can't you see? It's spider war!"

"But Ralphie…" said Alyssa,
"There is something you should know.
That's not the one I screamed about,
That's not the one…oh, no…"

"What?" quivered Ralphie,
As he suddenly felt colder.
A giant, slimy, hairy leg
Had tapped him on the shoulder.

"Hello!" came a booming voice
As Ralphie jumped with fear.
He turned and saw a spider,
Six feet wide from ear to ear!

Ralphie's eyes went blank,
His arms fell limp down to his side.
The spider flashed a silly grin,
Eight eyes were growing wide.

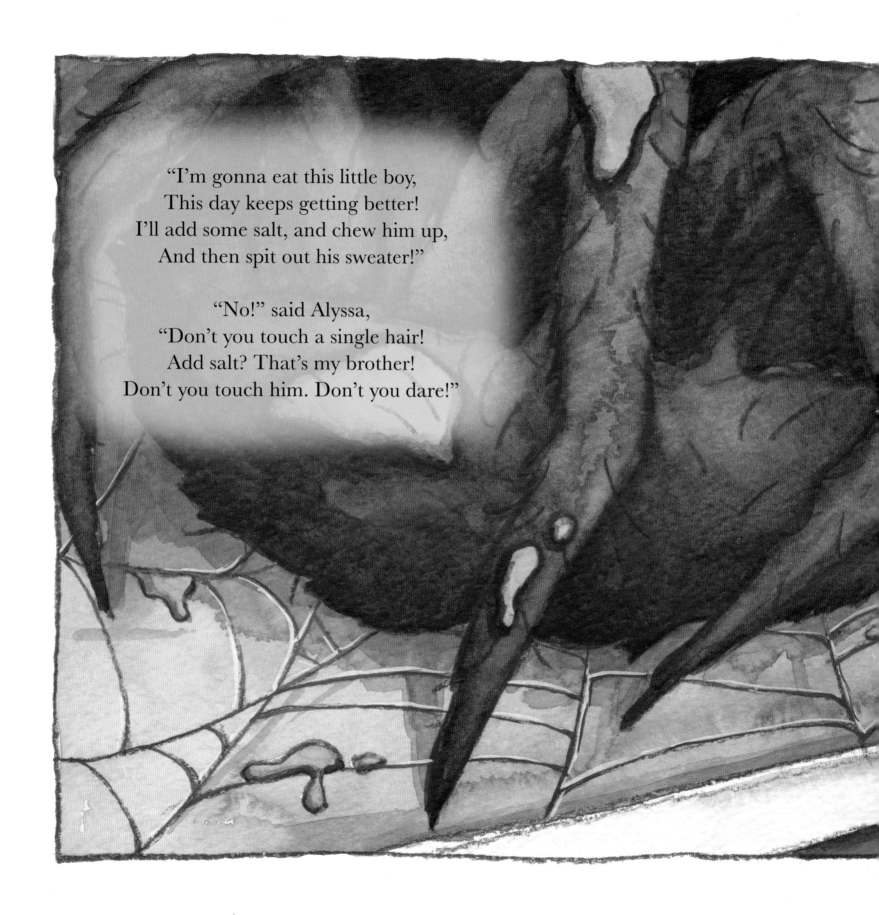

"I'm gonna eat this little boy,
This day keeps getting better!
I'll add some salt, and chew him up,
And then spit out his sweater!"

"No!" said Alyssa,
"Don't you touch a single hair!
Add salt? That's my brother!
Don't you touch him. Don't you dare!"

Ralphie started shaking,
Then, everything went dark.
He thought he heard Alyssa,
Did he hear a spider bark?

"Wake up! Wake up!" her voice again,
He opened up his eyes.
"Ralphie, you've been dreaming
Was it bad? I heard your cries…"

Ralphie coughed and rubbed his eyes,
Then stumbled down the hall.
When he returned, his arms were full,
"I think I found them all!"

"It's Jibby, Jack and Jume!"
Alyssa squealed with sheer delight.
Ralphie got a sewing kit
And worked on Jibby's sight.

"You're my favorite sister."
Whispered Ralphie from the floor.

Then He Winked

"You know, I like you more
Than all the candy at the store."